THE BOY WITH THE
HELIUM HEAD

THE BOY WITH THE
HELIUM HEAD

Phyllis Reynolds Naylor
Illustrated by Kay Chorao

A Yearling First Choice Chapter Book

*For Catherine and Mary Archibald
and their parents* —P.R.N.

Published by
Bantam Doubleday Dell Publishing Group, Inc.
1540 Broadway
New York, New York 10036

Previously published as a Young Yearling Book by Dell Publishing,
a division of Bantam Doubleday Dell

Library of Congress Cataloging-in-Publication Data
ISBN: 0-440-41498-9
Cataloging-in-Publication Data is available from the Library of Congress.

The trademark Yearling® is registered in the U.S. Patent and Trademark
Office and in other countries.

Visit us on the Web! www.bdd.com
Educators and librarians, visit the BDD Teacher's Resource Center at
www.bdd.com/teachers

The text of this book is set in 17-point Baskerville.
Manufactured in the United States of America
August 1998
10 9 8 7 6 5 4 3 2

CONTENTS

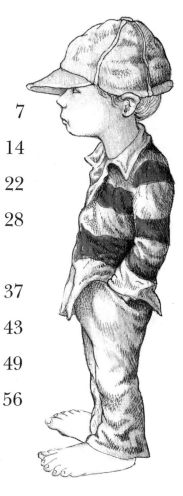

1.
A ROTTEN DAY

It was going to be one of those days.
Jonathan could feel it as soon as
he saw what they were having
for breakfast.
"Not Cream of Wheat!" he said.

He could tell by the way Baby Sam
frowned at him from across the table.
"Glumpf da da," said Baby Sam.
He knew it when his mother said,
"This is the day
for flu shots, Jonathan."
And he was sure of it when he
remembered that Duke Duncan was
going to beat the daylights out of him
for sitting on his sandwich.

It was a tuna fish sandwich,
Duke Duncan's favorite kind.
"I didn't mean to sit on it,"
Jonathan had said.

That didn't make any difference.
Duke was eight years old, and big.
Jonathan was only seven, and
wore size small in everything
except his shoes.
His feet, in fact, were extra large.
"I feel like a chipmunk wearing
snowshoes," he said once.
When he put on his cap, which
fell down over his eyes, Jonathan
decided he had been put together
all wrong.

Baby Sam was huge. He was so big
that he already wore
Jonathan's T-shirts.

He was so fat that he could hardly
squeeze into his high chair.
And he was so loud that whenever he
opened his giant mouth, his mother
came running at once.

11

Jonathan slowly went upstairs
to brush his teeth. Even his
toothbrush was extra small.
He had to stand on a stepstool
to reach the faucet.
"I'll bet Duke Duncan doesn't get
flu shots," Jonathan said to himself.
"Duke Duncan doesn't even
brush his teeth!"
Half the town was sick with flu, but
Duke Duncan wouldn't catch it.
Duke Duncan was big and strong
and mean and lucky. As soon as he
caught Jonathan alone, he was
going to beat him up. That's the
kind of day it would be.

2.
THE BAD BABY

There were only two nice things
about going to Dr. Mack.
First, Baby Sam had to get
a flu shot too.

14

Second, the doctor had promised
a helium balloon
to every boy and girl who came in.
Jonathan and his mother and Baby
Sam went to the doctor's office.
There was a long line waiting.

Each time a child passed by, Dr. Mack
shot medicine into his arm, helium into
a balloon, and sent him happily home.
That was before Baby Sam
got in line, however.

Baby Sam did not like to sit
in his stroller. He began to bang
his fist hard on the wall.
One of the nurses frowned.
Jonathan's mother sang
a song to Baby Sam.
He only pounded harder.
"Please make him stop," said
another nurse. She put
her hands over her ears.
Jonathan and his mother tried to
play pat-a-cake and peekaboo with
the huge baby, but Baby Sam
stomped his feet.
"Please, *please* make that child be
quiet," said all the nurses together.

Finally they rushed the Bogleys to
the head of the line to get them out
of the office.

Baby Sam took one look
at Dr. Mack and howled.
He waved his fat arms
and kicked his huge legs.
He knocked over the tray of needles
and sent the doctor's glasses flying.
Jonathan tried hard not to laugh.
He tried to act as though he had
never seen Baby Sam before
in his life.

"Is this the way your brother is at home?" one of the nurses asked Jonathan.

"What brother?" said Jonathan.

Old Dr. Mack had to sit on Sammy to give him the shot, and finally handed the baby a red balloon. But Sammy was not happy with just one balloon. He wanted more. Even when Dr. Mack gave him a yellow one, too, Baby Sam wouldn't shut up. He yelled so loudly that other children began to cry.

Dr. Mack was in a great hurry to get
Jonathan's family out of his office.
When Jonathan stepped up in line,
the doctor shot helium into
Jonathan's arm by mistake,
put medicine in the balloon, and
led the Bogleys to the door.

3.
JONATHAN RISES

Outside, Jonathan noticed
that his balloon was not rising.
Sammy's balloons, however,
bobbed high overhead.

"Just my luck!" Jonathan thought.
"What a stinking, rotten day!"
A rotten day, a stupid balloon, a
lousy shot, and a screaming baby.
That was his life.

At the same time, however,
he began to feel very odd indeed.
He followed along behind his
mother, but something seemed to be
wrong with his feet. They hardly
touched the sidewalk at all.
Jonathan stared down at his shoes.
He carefully put one foot
in front of the other.
Now he was sure of it!
Yes! He was rising!

Suddenly a big hand grabbed hold of
Jonathan's arm. A big voice said,
"I've been looking for you,

Jonathan Bogley. I'm going to teach you something about sitting on a sandwich."

There stood Duke Duncan with his two big fists in front of his chest.

At that moment, however, Jonathan rose. Duke's right fist came forward, but Jonathan was not there.

Duke Duncan went spinning around and around.

On Jonathan went until he was even with the telephone wires. Then he stopped and dangled strangely in the air.

Duke Duncan stared up at him, his mouth open.

A crowd gathered below. Jonathan saw his mother turn around. She came rushing back up the sidewalk at full speed. The wheels of Sammy's stroller spun madly. "Jonathan!" she cried.

"Come down at once!"

"I can't!" Jonathan said, more surprised than scared. No matter how he twisted and turned, he went right on bobbing about in the air. Duke Duncan stood below, watching.

4.
SMEDLEY, WHOOPLE, AND FIZZ

The fire department arrived, sirens wailing, followed by the rescue squad and a police helicopter.

The firemen put up a ladder, and Jonathan climbed down. As soon as he got to the bottom and let go, however, he shot right back up. The police helicopter lowered a rope ladder and pulled Jonathan up. But as soon as it landed and Jonathan got out, back up he went again!

Old Dr. Mack heard all the noise and came out of his office. He was very surprised to see one of the Bogleys floating there above the First National Bank.

"Bring Jonathan down again so that
I can take a look at him,"
he told the rescue squad.
Jonathan came down the ladder
once more.
Dr. Mack looked in his ears.
"I don't believe it!" he said.
He called out to the three doctors
who worked next door—
Drs. Smedley, Whoople, and Fizz.

They shone flashlights up
Jonathan's nose. They thumped
him on the back and
tapped his knees.

Finally they picked him up by the heels and shook him up and down. Dr. Mack turned to Jonathan's mother.

"My dear Mrs. Bogley," he said. "I am afraid what we have here is a case of helium in the head." Drs. Smedley, Whoople, and Fizz nodded gravely.

"Actually," said Dr. Smedley, "this has never happened before in all of medical history."

Jonathan, whom they had let go of, was floating once more. He clicked his heels in midair and turned a cartwheel above the fire station.

"I have heard of water in the ears and gas in the stomach, but never helium in the head," said Dr. Whoople.

"A very strange case indeed!" agreed Dr. Fizz. "If it were not for his feet, which *are* rather large, he might go right on rising, and who knows where he might end?"

"Do you mean," asked Mrs. Bogley, beginning to weep, "that my Jonathan is to spend the rest of his life rising and falling like a barometer?"

"Not likely," said Dr. Mack. "The helium is slowly coming out of his ears. By tomorrow evening it should

34

all be gone. But I want him
to do as I say."
Dr. Mack wrote something on a
pad of paper. He gave it to
Jonathan, who had climbed down
the telephone pole himself.

Jonathan was careful to stay around people so that Duke Duncan could not catch him alone.

The piece of paper said:

No crawling in chimneys.
Obey all traffic signals.
Watch for low ceilings.

"Also, drink plenty of water and keep your shirt on," said Drs. Smedley, Whoople, and Fizz.

5.
THE BOY IN THE AIR

No one knew what to do while
Jonathan had helium in his head.
"I do not know what to tell you,
Mrs. Bogley," said old Dr. Mack,
"but he should be kept as
comfortable as possible."

Jonathan said he would like
to stay outside.

"I don't want to be tied to my bed to
keep me from rising," he told his
mother. "But I certainly do not want to
spend the time pressed against
the ceiling of my room."

The day was warm and the sky was
clear, so Mrs. Bogley said
he could stay outdoors.

Jonathan decided to make the most of
this strange situation. He walked
along the telephone wires,
balancing carefully. When he slipped
off, he simply bobbed back on again.

There below him was Duke Duncan,
watching.

Next Jonathan skimmed the roofs of
all the shops on the block.
He dropped down a kite he had found
twisted around a chimney. He threw
down a ball that was stuck
in a rain gutter.

When he came to the end of the
shops on the street, he stepped off
and walked through the air to
the roofs on the other side.
Duke Duncan tagged along below,
saying nothing.

When he got to the park, Jonathan
air-walked to the trees and bobbed
about in the branches.

He peeped into birds' nests and
startled the squirrels.

But whenever he looked down,
there was Duke Duncan.

"How about a game of baseball,
Jonathan?" some friends called.
"You can play center field."
When a batter hit a ball high
in the air, Jonathan caught it.
Jonathan's team won.
They played basketball next. When
Jonathan had the ball, he simply
bobbed over to the basket and
dropped the ball inside.
"This is the life!" he thought.
"No Duke Duncan, no Baby Sam."
He began to wish he could go on
like this forever.

6.
A NIGHT IN THE SKY

That evening, Mrs. Bogley said,
"Jonathan, play with Sammy, please.
I want to make dinner."
Jonathan came into the house. He
walked upside down on the ceiling.

Baby Sam laughed and waved
his fat arms.

Mrs. Bogley made a chicken pie and
a salad. Jonathan ate them outside,
sitting high on a church steeple.
He waved to the airplanes that passed.
He called hello to the people below.
When he found an olive in his salad,
he simply spit it out. There was
no one to tell him what to do.

As evening fell, Jonathan bobbed
around in the air until dark.
A light came on in Dr. Mack's house
as he passed. Dr. Mack, Jonathan
discovered, wore a wig.

A light came on in the mayor's house.
The mayor, Jonathan saw,
had false teeth.
As he bobbed by Duke Duncan's
house, Jonathan looked through the
window. He saw Duke in his room.
Duke had on a pair of boxing gloves.
Jonathan swallowed.

When it was time for bed, Jonathan's
mother gave him a blanket and pillow.
He went to sleep above the clock
at city hall.
Jonathan dreamed that Duke Duncan
had crawled up the side of the

building in the night and
was about to slug him.

When he woke the next morning,
Jonathan found that he had rolled
about quite a bit. He had rolled
several blocks, in fact.

His blanket was tangled in the
weather vane above the post office.
And there below was Duke Duncan,
waiting. Jonathan tried not to think
about what would happen
when he came down.

7.
HELPING THE MAYOR

The newspaper had Jonathan's picture
on the front page. The radio carried
his story on the morning news.

The local TV station sent out a crew.
They taped Jonathan
eating breakfast on a flagpole.
"Maybe the doctors were wrong,"
Jonathan said to himself.
Perhaps the helium would stay in
his head a long time. Forever, even.
Maybe he would be the first boy
to live his life on a flagpole.
If he lived in the air, he could
cross streets without looking.
He could watch football games
without buying a ticket.
He would have the very best seat
to watch fireworks on the
Fourth of July.

All he had to do when he wanted to go
down was to grab hold of a drainpipe
or telephone pole and lower himself
to the ground.

The mayor thought of all kinds of
things that Jonathan could do
for the city.
"Would you change the burned-out
bulbs in the streetlights?"
he wanted to know.
Jonathan did.
"Would you paint the steeple?" he asked.
"Gladly," said Jonathan.
"String up some lights for us," said

someone else. "Polish a bell."

"Shingle a roof."

"Hook up a clothesline."

"Trim a tree."

There were more and more jobs to
do for a boy who could walk on air.
Some space scientists came from
Washington. They wanted to see if
Jonathan could put on his socks and
shoes while bobbing about overhead.
They wanted to know if he could
drink a milk shake upside down.
"Chocolate, please," said Jonathan.
And he did just fine.

He even saw some robbers, running
out of the bank. Because he was high
in the air, he saw where they went.
He told the police. The robbers
were soon in jail.

"Wonderful job!" said the chief of
police. "Wonderful job indeed!"

If only the fun would last.

8.
COMING DOWN

By two that afternoon, however,
before he had done half the things he
wanted to, Jonathan began to sink.
By three he was no higher than
the fir trees.

By four he was as low as
the roof of his house.
By five he had reached the window
frames, and by six his feet were
touching the ground.

Duke Duncan was there, but so was
a brass band. Jonathan was given a
ride around town on the fire truck.
Baby Sam waved one fat fist at him
from his stroller.
For dinner that evening
Mrs. Bogley made chocolate soup,
mashed potatoes with chocolate
gravy, chocolate meatballs, and for

dessert, a big chocolate layer cake topped with chocolate ice cream and chocolate fudge sauce.

They listened to the story of the boy with the helium head on the evening news. They saw the tape of the parade, with Jonathan waving at the crowd.

On Monday, however, everyone seemed to have forgotten about Jonathan. The newspapers had been thrown out with the morning trash.

The brass band was playing in another town.

The TV was talking about Texas and taxes. Jonathan Bogley was just another boy with big feet.
But Duke Duncan didn't forget.
When Jonathan got to school,
Duke was waiting.

When Jonathan sat down,

Duke sat down.

When Jonathan stood up,

Duke stood up.

Wherever Jonathan went,

Duke followed.

And to everyone they met, Duke said proudly, "I was the very first one to see him go up! Honest! And to think that *he*—Jonathan Bogley—actually sat on my sandwich!"

Phyllis Reynolds Naylor used to dream that she could fly just by flapping her arms up and down. And sometimes dreams become books, only they are changed a little in the making. Mrs. Naylor is the author of ninety books for children, including *Shiloh,* winner of the Newbery Award. She lives in Bethesda, Maryland, with her husband, Rex.

Kay Chorao is an award-winning artist who has written and illustrated many books, including *The Book of Giving* and *Jumpety-Bumpety Hop.*